Contents

Red Bananas

SUGAR

MONTY WINS THE CUP

by JAKE SPARKS

Illustrated by Kimberley Scott

For Mia – J.S.

For my Big Sister Joey – K.S.

With special thanks to
Barry Hutchison

EGMONT
We bring stories to life

Book Band: Purple

First published in Great Britain 2012
by Egmont UK Ltd
The Yellow Building, 1 Nicholas Road, London W11 4AN

ISBN 978 1 4052 5949 1
10 9 8 7 6 5 4 3 2 1
A CIP catalogue record for this title is available from the British Library.
Printed in Singapore.
49136/1

A Birthday Surprise

Danny Crankshaft yawned, stretched and opened his eyes. He lay in bed for a few seconds, then he remembered what day it was and sat up suddenly.

'My birthday!' he cheered. He kicked off the covers and jumped out of bed. 'Today's my birthday!'

Danny ran down the stairs two at a time. His mum and dad were sitting at the kitchen table, waiting for a steam-powered machine to finish buttering their toast. Danny's dad liked to come up with ideas for inventions, and Danny's mum liked to build them.

Their house was full of strange machines that clanked and whirred and did everything from cleaning the windows to boiling eggs for breakfast. Most of the time the machines worked perfectly. Most of the time, but not always.

'Here's the birthday boy!' said Mr Crankshaft. He clapped his hands excitedly, then he ducked as a slice of buttered toast whizzed past above his head.

'We've made you a special birthday breakfast,' said Mrs Crankshaft. 'Chocolate milkshake and a jelly-baby sandwich.'

'Wahoo!' cried Danny. He loved chocolate milkshakes. He had never had a jelly-baby sandwich before, but it sounded brilliant.

'Here's your card,' said Mr Crankshaft, handing Danny a white envelope covered with oily smudges.

Danny tore open the envelope. Inside was a card with the words 'HAPPY BIRTHDAY' written across it in big, bold letters. There was something else in the envelope too. It was a shiny silver key.

‘What’s this for?’ Danny asked.

‘Look outside,’ said his mum.

Danny ran to the back door and dashed out into the garden, still wearing his pyjamas.

Then he stopped.

Then he stared.

Then he gave a great cheer of excitement.

Down at the end of the path was a racing car. It didn't look like any ordinary racing car, though. The doors were a different colour to the bumpers, and the bumpers didn't match the bonnet. It looked as if it had been built using bits from a hundred different cars. It was dented in places, and the paint was peeling here and there. Danny loved it!

‘Happy birthday, son,’ said his mum and dad together. He raced over and gave them both a hug.

‘Have you remembered that it’s the day of the Tooting Wallop Road Race?’ Mrs Crankshaft asked.

‘Of course!’ said Danny. ‘Can we go and watch it as a birthday treat? Please!’

Mr Crankshaft laughed. ‘Watch it?’ he said. ‘You’re going to *race* in it!’

The Test Drive

Danny whooped with delight and ran down the path to the little car. He jumped into the driver's seat and turned the silver key. The car made a noise, but the engine didn't start.

'There's something wrong,' Danny said. 'Does it need petrol?'

'Ah, no, it doesn't run on petrol,' said Mr Crankshaft. 'This car's just like you, Danny. It runs on . . .'

'Chocolate milkshake!' cried Danny.

In a flash, he ran back into the house. He returned a moment later carrying his milkshake. There was a big glass bottle at the back of the car. Danny poured the milkshake in and watched it swirl around inside.

When it was full, the car made a noise that sounded a bit like a burp. Danny jumped back into the driver's seat.

'Wait for us,' laughed his dad. Mr and Mrs Crankshaft squeezed into the back seat. All three of them carefully did up their seat belts, then Danny turned the key.

VROOOOOOM!

The engine roared. Danny and his parents cheered.

‘Let’s try driving it around the garden,’ Mr Crankshaft suggested. ‘Nice and slow to begin with, don’t go too *faaaaaaaaaaast*!’

Danny pushed his foot down on the ‘go’ pedal and the car shot forwards – straight towards the garden hedge!

‘Look out!’ yelped Mrs Crankshaft, covering her eyes with her oily hands.

Danny pulled the wheel and the car turned in a tight circle around a garden gnome, just missing the hedge. The tyres spun for a second, and then the car sped across the grass.

'Wow!' Danny cried, patting the dashboard. 'You're amazing!'

VROOOM, went the car. The chocolate milkshake in the bottle at the back began to bubble and gurgle. *VROOOM-VROOOOOM!*

Danny laughed. 'That almost sounded like you were talking to me,' he said.

BEEP, went the car's horn. *BEEP-BEEEEEEP!* 'He *was* talking to you,' Mr Crankshaft said.

'It's our special boy's seventh birthday,' said Mrs Crankshaft. 'And we thought he deserved a special car.'

'What are you going to call him?' asked Mr Crankshaft. 'I thought "Whizzy".'

'Or "Speedy",' suggested Mrs Crankshaft.

'Monty,' said Danny. 'I'm calling him Monty.'

Monty gave a happy *peep* of his horn, and the milkshake in the back bubbled some more.

'I think he likes it,' Danny said. 'Can we do another lap?'

'No time,' said his dad. 'You have to get dressed. The race will be starting any minute!'

The Race Begins

The town of Tooting Wallop was buzzing with excitement. The Tooting Wallop Road Race was open to everyone, no matter how young or old they were. The oldest person in the race was Granny Atkins. She had been racing for sixty-seven years, and she had come second every single time.

Granny Atkins and the other racers were already lining up in their cars at the start when Danny drove up in Monty. Two of his friends from school, James and Priti, were also racing this year. They gave him a friendly wave as he came to a stop.

'Hello, Danny,' said James.

'What's that you've got?' asked Priti. 'Is it a new car?'

‘It looks more like a junk yard on wheels,’ said one of the spectators with a nasty laugh.

Danny patted the bonnet. ‘Don’t listen, Monty,’ he said. ‘You’re better than any car here.’

Monty gave a soft *vroom* in reply, but the growling of another engine drowned the sound out. A shadow fell over Monty as a much larger car pulled up beside him. The car was dark purple, with red flames painted along the side.

Danny and his parents looked up at the bigger car. A face they all recognised shot a dirty look back at them.

'Oh no!' Danny muttered. 'It's Hugo de Horrible!'

'Horrible by name . . .' whispered Mrs Crankshaft.

'. . . and horrible by nature,' said Mr Crankshaft.

Hugo's electric window slid open. He twirled his black moustache and peered down his nose at the smaller car.

'You don't seriously plan on driving that thing, do you?' he sneered. 'I'm going to win the Road Race and take home the Tooting Wallop Cup. That rust-bucket has no chance.'

'Just you wait and see,' said Danny. 'He might not be as big or shiny, but Monty's just as good as your car.'

Hugo de Horrible laughed loudly. 'My car is the fastest in the whole of Tooting Wallop, and the most expensive. That thing looks like it was made in a shed.'

'It *was* made in a shed,' said Mr Crankshaft.

'Ha!' sniggered Hugo. 'Precisely!'

PEEP! went Monty's horn angrily. His windscreen wipers flicked on and a spray of chocolate milkshake shot out – right into Hugo's face!

Danny giggled. 'Whoops. Sorry!'

Monty's engine gave a little gurgle that sounded like a giggle of his own.

'You'll pay for that,' spluttered Hugo, wringing milkshake out of his moustache. 'I'll make sure of it.'

The red starting lights began to flash. Danny looked at his parents, who were still squashed together in the back seat. 'Good luck, Danny,' Mrs Crankshaft said.

'You can do it!' added Mr Crankshaft.

Danny gripped the steering wheel. 'Ready, Monty?' Monty revved his engine in reply. 'Good. Let's show them all what you can do!'

The lights turned green. Danny pushed down on the 'go' pedal and Monty zoomed forwards, ahead of all the other cars. They were going to take the lead!

Suddenly, Hugo de Horrible deliberately steered his car right into Monty's path. Danny swerved sharply to avoid him and –

CRASH!

Monty smashed into a lamp post and came to a stop.

'I told you I'd make you pay for squirting me,' laughed Hugo, as he led the other cars around the first bend, leaving Monty far behind.

A Quick Fix

'Is he going to be OK?' asked Danny nervously.

'Is he badly damaged?' said Mr Crankshaft.

All three members of the Crankshaft family were down on their knees, looking at the big dent in Monty's bonnet.

'He's going to be fine,' said Mrs Crankshaft. She reached into her tool bag and pulled out a big sink plunger. The rubber suction cup on the end made a *shlop* noise as she pushed it against the dent. With a heave, she pulled.

Monty honked loudly as the dent popped back into place. He looked as good as new.

He gave a *vroom* of his engine and rolled forwards just a little. He couldn't wait to get back into the race.

'You're right,' said Danny. 'There's no time to lose!'

Danny and his parents jumped into the car and reversed away from the lamp post. Then, with a loud *VROOOOOOOOM*, Monty shot off after the other racers.

Danny skilfully steered Monty through the streets of Tooting Wallop.

ZOOM!

They passed the windmill where Doughy Simmons the baker lived.

WHOOSH!

They skidded past the duck pond. The ducks waved brightly coloured flags and quacked loudly as the car shot by.

WHIZZ!

They passed the wishing well, the giraffe shop and Stinky Cheese Hill. In no time at all, they caught up with the other racers. Monty *beep-beeped* happily as they raced past one car, then another, then another. James and Priti waved as Monty overtook them, and Danny waved back.

Danny and his parents cheered as they overtook Granny Atkins too. They had made it all the way to second place. There was only Hugo de Horrible to beat!

'You can do it, Monty!' Danny yelled.

'You're catching him!' cried Mr and Mrs Crankshaft.

Monty's engine revved loudly as he closed in on Hugo's car. Up in front, Hugo began to panic. He weaved across the road, trying to stop Monty overtaking him. He dodged left, then swung right. His wheels squealed as he skidded across the road.

Suddenly, the road turned sharply. Hugo tried to steer around the bend, but he was going too fast. With a final screech from the tyres, Hugo lost control of his car. It spun around in a wide circle and smashed through the side of the Tooting Wallop bridge. Hugo gave a yelp of fright as the car's back wheels rolled off the bridge, leaving him dangling over the edge!

The Rescue

'You're going to take the lead, Danny,' yelped Mr Crankshaft. 'Keep going!'

Danny pushed down harder on the 'go' pedal as they raced towards the bridge. But Monty didn't speed up. Instead, he began to slow down.

'What are you doing, Monty?' asked Danny. No matter how much he pressed down on the pedal, the little car refused to go faster. In fact, Monty was coming to a stop right beside Hugo's car.

'He's stopping. Why's he stopping?' asked Mrs Crankshaft.

'Maybe he's out of milkshake,' suggested Mr Crankshaft.

Danny looked back at the milkshake bottle. It was still half full.

Monty made his engine go *vroom*, and Danny realised what he was trying to tell them.

'We have to help Hugo,' Danny said. 'I know he's horrible, but if we just leave him, that means we're horrible too. We have to help him, even if he is a mean old misery guts.' Danny sighed. 'And even if it means losing the race.'

There was a cheerful *peep-peep* from Monty.

'You're right, Danny – and you too, Monty,' said Mr Crankshaft.

'Yes, we can't just leave him hanging there,' agreed Mrs Crankshaft.

'Help!' Hugo cried. 'I'm g-going to f-fall!'

'Don't worry,' shouted Danny, as he turned Monty around. 'This *rust-bucket* is going to save you. Mum, Dad – is there a rope or something I can pull him up with?'

Danny's dad smiled proudly. 'There's something better than that,' he said. 'See that red button beside the steering wheel?'

Danny found the button. 'Got it!'

The button went *bleep* as Danny pressed it. With a loud whirring noise, Monty's boot flew open and a huge mechanical hand reached out from inside. It caught hold of Hugo's car and Monty gave a *peep* to let Danny know he was ready.

Hold on!

'Monty, you're *amazing*,' laughed Danny.

Monty *vrooomed* to show he agreed. Then, with a roar from his engine, he pulled Hugo's car back on to the road, and they began the slow drive towards the finish line.

Across the Finish Line

A great cheer went up as Monty crawled around the final corner, pulling Hugo's car behind him. Danny looked around at the crowd, who were clapping and waving with delight.

'I don't understand,' Danny said. 'Why are they cheering? We're last.'

HONK-HONK, went Monty.

'You're right, Monty, we're not quite last,' Danny grinned. 'We're still going to beat Hugo!'

Danny looked back at the car they were towing. Hugo was bright red and squirming with embarrassment. He looked as if he had ants in his pants!

As Monty trundled over the finish line, the cheering became even louder. People rushed up to the little car, taking photographs and trying to shake Danny's hand.

'Ladies and gentlemen, the prize-giving is about to begin,' announced the mayor.

Danny and his parents climbed out of Monty and waved to the cheering crowd. 'You did great, Monty,' Danny whispered, giving the car a pat on the bonnet. Monty *beeped* happily in reply.

Danny and his parents joined the other drivers in a long line beside the mayor. James and Priti gave Danny a big smile. Granny Atkins straightened her glasses and polished

her false teeth on her sleeve. Everyone looked happy. Everyone except Hugo de Horrible, who stood right at the back of the line, scowling.

The mayor stepped up to the front of the crowd, holding an enormous gold cup. 'It gives me great pleasure to declare that this year's winner of the Tooting Wallop Cup is . . . Granny Atkins!' he boomed.

The mayor held out the cup to Granny Atkins, but the old lady shook her head.

'No,' said Granny Atkins firmly. 'I only won because Danny stopped to help Hugo. If anyone deserves the Tooting Wallop Cup it's Danny and Monty. They're the *real* winners.' She gave Danny a beaming smile. 'Besides, I like coming second.'

The crowd let out a huge cheer as the mayor passed the cup to Danny. Monty *VROOMED*

Tooting Wallop Road Race
Goodie!
Hooray!
1st
2nd
3rd

his engine loudly and Danny laughed. They had done it. They had won the Tooting Wallop Cup!

Danny patted Monty's steering wheel and the little car honked his horn merrily. 'You know, Monty,' Danny said, 'I think we're going to have lots more exciting adventures together.'

Monty gave another *peep-peep*. Danny was right. Their adventures had only just begun!